JOIN THE TEAM

Do you watch GHOSTWRITER on PBS? Then you know that when you read and write to solve a mystery or unravel a puzzle, you're using the same smarts and skills the Ghostwriter team uses.

We hope you'll join the team and read along to help solve the mysterious and puzzling goings-on in these GHOSTWRITER books!

BLACKOUT!

by Eric Weiner
illustrated by Eric Velasquez

A Children's Television Workshop Book

BANTAM BOOKS
NEW YORK • TORONTO • LONDON • SYDNEY • AUCKLAND

BLACKOUT!
A Bantam Book / December 1993

Ghostwriter, **Ghost**writer *and* 💣 *are
trademarks of Children's Television Workshop.
All rights reserved. Used under authorization.*

*Art direction by Marva Martin
Cover design by Susan Herr
Interior illustrations by Eric Velasquez*

ISBN 0-553-37302-1

Published simultaneously in the United States and Canada

*Bantam Books are published by Bantam Books, a division of Bantam
Doubleday Dell Publishing Group, Inc. Its trademark, consisting of the
words "Bantam Books" and the portrayal of a rooster, is Registered in U.S.
Patent and Trademark Office and in other countries. Marca Registrada.
Bantam Books, 1540 Broadway, New York, New York 10036.*

PRINTED IN THE UNITED STATES OF AMERICA

OPM   0   9   8   7   6   5   4   3

TERRIBLE TROUBLE!

"Hi! Gaby Fernandez here for the Washington School Video News. Check it out! I am standing here with the famous artist Quito Martinez! Or, as we all call him in the hood—Q!"

Gaby held her microphone toward Q. "What's happening?" said Q with a grin.

It was a cloudy Monday afternoon in winter. Gaby and Q were standing in the middle of the sidewalk on Harris Boulevard in Brooklyn. A few yards away stood Tina, filming the action with their school's video camera. The sidewalk was busy. They had already stopped the interview twice, thanks to people walking by and blocking the picture.

"Wait a minute," Tina called.

Gaby frowned. "Uh-oh. Now what?"

"The little red light isn't going on," Tina said, carefully studying the camera.

"Great," said Gaby. "C'mon, it looks like it's going to rain any minute."

"Just a sec," Tina said.

"Please stand by," Gaby told Q. "We are experiencing technical difficulties."

"Happens to me all the time," Q said, chuckling.

"There," called Tina almost at once. "I'm all set now."

"And now back to our regularly scheduled broadcast," said Gaby with a smile. "First of all, Q, I want to thank you for taking the time to talk to us. I know you're a very busy person."

"*De nada*," Q said. "That's Spanish for 'it's nothing.'"

Gaby's face lit up. "You speak Spanish? *¿Habla Usted Español?*" She started rattling off a stream of Spanish.

"Whoa, whoa!" Q held up his hand. "I know a few phrases, but . . ."

"Oh, sorry," Gaby said. "My parents are from El Salvador and—"

"Gaby. Gaby! *Gaby!* The interview?" Tina prompted from behind the camera.

"Right." Gaby gazed into the camera. "You may be wondering how we got to talk to Q. Well, we spotted him doing a mural near the park last week, and when we asked him, he agreed right away. Which just shows you that not all people who get famous become snobs."

Q laughed. "Thanks."

Gaby turned and pointed at the huge mural painted on the three-story building behind them. "As you can see, we're standing in front of one of Q's works right now."

The mural showed a large apartment building in flames. The people in the picture—people of all races and colors—had formed a human chain and were magically holding back the fire. Set into the middle of the mural was a list of names—these were innocent people who had been victims of crimes in Fort Greene, Brooklyn.

"THE FORT IS BURNING," blazed the mural's title. "AND ONLY WE CAN PUT OUT THE FLAMES." In the lower right corner was a slashing signature, the famous purple Q.

"Can you explain this picture for us?" Gaby asked.

"Yeah, sure. I guess I'd say it's about teamwork," answered Q. "We read about so many problems here in Fort Greene— poverty, drugs, crime, kids dropping out of school, people who can't read. I wanted to show that if we all stick together and work together, instead of fighting each other, then we can change things."

Gaby nodded. "Tina," she called, "are you getting all of the mural?"

"I think so," came Tina's reply from behind the camera.

"Q has a show on right now at the Brooklyn Museum," Gaby said to the camera. "So all of you who think museums are just full of boring old paintings should check it out. Uh, how much do your paintings sell for now, Q?"

"Around ten thousand dollars apiece," Q said, "if you can believe that."

Gaby's mouth dropped open. "Wow! So why do you still live around here? I mean, with all the money you must have, you could live someplace really fancy."

"I was born here," Q said. "I grew up right here in Fort Greene. I'm not going to be one of those guys who takes his money and runs. I want to do what I can to hold this place together."

Q was in his mid-thirties, thin and wiry, with dark, shiny eyes. You could tell just by looking at him what he did for a living. His black denims, his gray hooded sweatshirt, and even his black hair were all streaked with Day-Glo spray paint, every color of the rainbow.

Gaby noticed that Tina had started to back away across the wide sidewalk. Where was she going? "Ah, how did you get started doing spray-paint art?" Gaby asked Q.

"I had always been into painting," he answered. "Then when I was your age, my father's little hardware store was broken into. I came home from school and he was crying. The whole place was trashed, stuff lying all over the floor. I saw these cans of spray paint, and I took one and ran out of there. I found this store with a big blank wall, you know? And I painted the word HATE as big as I could.

"But while I was painting it, the storekeeper came running out and grabbed me. It turned out to be Xavier Ruiz, one of my father's best friends. As a punishment, Mr. Ruiz told me I would have to paint over that word HATE with a picture that would make people feel better instead of worse.

"That was my very first mural. Everyone liked that mural so much, they started hiring me to do pictures on *their* stores, and then the city hired me to do pictures in the subways. I've never stopped working since."

Great story! thought Gaby. She was so glad she'd asked that question. The interview was going great. She checked her list of written questions. "So," she said, "a lot of us kids have been wondering: How did you get the name Quito?"

"My parents came to this country from Quito, Ecuador," Q explained. "Quito's the capital, and they wanted me always to remember where I'm from. . . . "

Gaby stopped listening. Q was going on about life in Quito, but Gaby didn't hear a word. Instead, she was staring in horror at her friend Tina. Still filming, and still squinting through the camera, Tina was now backing out into the street.

Right in front of an oncoming truck.

Gaby opened her mouth to scream a warning. But she was frozen with fear. And the words didn't come.

For Gaby, time now seemed to go into slow motion.

She saw Tina stop short—right in the middle of the street. Saw her take the camera away from her eye. Saw her begin studying it intently. Saw the truck barreling toward her.

At the same time, Tina was studying the instructions on the side of her camera—LOAD FILM THIS SIDE UP! Five of the letters in the message had rearranged themselves to form a flashing message:

UPSET!

Ghostwriter! was the thought that raced through Tina's head.

Ghostwriter, their invisible friend, couldn't see or hear. He could only read and write. But Tina knew that Ghostwriter could sense danger. And when Tina looked up from the camera, she saw the UPSET! Ghostwriter was writing about. It was Gaby. She looked as if she were about to throw up or something.

Tina turned.

She saw the truck zooming at her.

Just then Gaby shrieked, *"Tina!"*

7

CHAPTER 2

WHERE WERE YOU WHEN THE LIGHTS WENT OUT?

Tina dove backward. She landed on her back, still holding the camera. The truck's brakes squealed. The huge mass of hot metal and air was blasting right by her body.

A moment later, Gaby appeared above her. She was peering down at her, yelling, "What's the matter with you?"

"Am I all in one piece?" Tina asked, afraid to look.

"You are, but you're very lucky," Q said, helping her to her feet. "C'mon, let's get out of the street."

"What were you doing?" Gaby asked her once they were on the sidewalk.

"I was trying to get all of Q's mural in the shot," Tina explained sheepishly. "That was a little close, wasn't it?"

"You scared me to death, *mi amiga*," said Q, using the Spanish for "my friend."

Trying to slow her heart, Tina took several deep breaths. "All right," she said. "I'm okay."

"Well, I'm not," Gaby said.

Q laughed. "You're breathing harder than your friend."

"Sorry," Tina said again. She dusted off the back of her corduroy pants. Wanting to change the subject quickly, she glanced up at the sky, which was getting darker and more threatening by the minute. Then she checked her watch—4:22 P.M. She looked at her neatly typed schedule. "Well," she said. "I guess we should be moving along."

"Why?" joked Gaby. "What's next on the schedule? Getting hit by a train?"

Tina made an annoyed face. "No," she said. "Q, you said if there was time, you could show us some of your new art?"

"*Sí*," said Q with a nod. "I have a studio at the museum. We can go there now—as long as we can catch this bus!"

The bus had pulled into a stop about half a block away. Q and the two girls started to run. The bus started to pull out again, but Q rapped on the door and the driver stopped. The door wheezed open to let them on.

"Another close call," Q told Gaby and Tina. "Looks like today's our lucky day."

Which was when the first big drops of rain slashed hard against the bus windows.

At that exact same moment, on a wide, busy street, a blue truck had just pulled up next to a manhole. CON EDISON, said the white letters on the truck's side—New York's power company. Two workers in blue uniforms got out. One man was tall and heavy, the other short and skinny.

The workers set up yellow CAUTION, MEN WORKING signs around the manhole. First the big, tall man hammered at the edge of the manhole with a chisel. Then the skinny man wedged a crowbar under the manhole's thick metal lip. He pulled on the crowbar with all his might.

Nothing happened.

The heavy man threw back his head and laughed. He had a very deep voice. Then he shoved the skinny man out of the way. He yanked back hard on the crowbar, easily prying open the manhole cover. He pried it open so easily, in fact, that he bonked himself in the head with the crowbar's handle.

Now it was the skinny man's turn to laugh. But one look from the heavy man and he stopped laughing.

Glancing around to see if anyone was watching, the two workers climbed down into the manhole and disappeared underground.

"What did I tell you?" said the heavy man as they headed through a dark underground tunnel. "This is going to be a piece of cake."

Then he turned the corner. His jaw dropped.

The tunnel had widened into a huge room. The room was filled with electronic panels. There were blinking lights everywhere. There were also wires of all colors, and one whole row of large machines shaped in coils. The whole room was buzzing, like some giant snake about to strike.

"Oh no," said the skinny man in his high voice.

"Oh no, what?" demanded the heavy man.

"You know what this is?"

"This is where the main cable is," the big man said. "The cable that brings in electrical power for the street."

"No," said the small man. "This is what's known as a transmission center. I asked you about this, remember? You were supposed to check. Con Ed uses this place to send electric power all over the area."

The heavy man looked confused. "So?"

"So now we'll never figure out which wire to pull."

"Nonsense," said the heavy man. "You get scared too easily."

The skinny man pulled a chart out of his pocket. He unfolded it. He stared at it hopelessly. "Oh, oh, oh," he murmured.

"Never mind that!" snarled the heavy man, knocking the chart out of his coworker's hands. It fell to the floor. "The wire we're looking for is blue." The tall man pointed to a blue wire. "There. Yank it."

"Yank it?" The little man's eyebrows shot up. "Are you sure I should?"

The heavy man glowered. "Of course I'm sure."

"You were also sure this wasn't a transmission center."

The heavy man slapped a pair of pliers into the small man's hands. "Yank it."

"Why do I have to do it?" the little man asked. But he closed the teeth of the pliers around the blue wire. He blinked. He had started sweating.

And then he yanked.

Meanwhile, in a recording studio in downtown Brooklyn, Lenni Frazier was asking for more bass.

"Lenni," said the frizzy-haired bass guitarist, Fran Mc-Lanahan, "I've already got it turned up to eight."

"I know," Lenni said. "But I really want this song to have some punch, you know? I want it to be one of those songs that makes you feel your own heartbeat."

Fran laughed. "Okay," she said, clicking the amplifier up another notch. "You're the boss."

It was true, Lenni thought. She *was* the boss! For one hour, anyway. Her dad, Max, had been out of town playing a jazz gig on her last birthday. Well, he had made it up to her in a big way. As a belated birthday present, Max had "borrowed" a recording studio for her from some friends who were music producers. Max had asked Keith and Fran to help Lenni record one of her own songs.

Lenni stood under the large silver microphone that hung down from the ceiling. She adjusted the headphones over her ears. Then she signaled the technician, Keith, who was sitting at the control panel behind the glass window. For the sixth time that hour, she started to sing her song. The bass was booming. She swung her head to the beat, singing, "If your heart beats the message, then the message is true . . ."

She stopped again. She removed the headphones. Fran kept playing for a moment. Then she stopped as well. "Lenni," Fran said wearily. "You're worse than your father, you know that?"

"I guess that's where I get it from," Lenni admitted, blushing.

"We're running out of time here, kiddo," Fran said.

"I know, I'm really sorry." Lenni twisted a lock of her light brown hair. "But it's still not enough bass."

"It only goes one notch higher."

"Please?" Lenni begged. She didn't want to be a pain. Fran

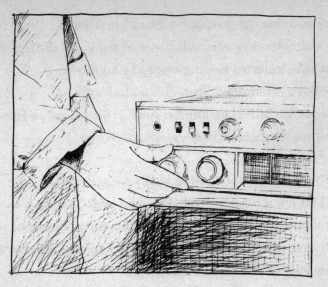

and Keith were doing her a huge favor. But she wanted her song to sound just right.

"Okay . . ." Sighing, Fran reached down and clicked the dial one last notch—to ten. She thumbed a low note. There was a sound like thunder.

Instantly all the lights in the studio went out.

"Uh-oh," said Lenni.

"Great," said Fran. "We just blew the power!"

In the dark booth, Lenni saw Keith's jaw drop. He pointed past her, out the window. Lenni turned and gasped. "Oh no!" She clapped both hands to her head. "I'm sorry! I'm sorry!"

From top to bottom, the lights were draining out of the tall office buildings of downtown Brooklyn. Though it was only late afternoon, it was a dark day, and rainy. As all the lights went out, it started looking more like nighttime.

"Wow," murmured Fran. "It's a blackout!"

Lenni was still clutching her head as she turned to Fran. "I guess you were right, that *was* too much bass!"

The dentist's drill whirred loudly.

"You know what?" Alex Fernandez said. "Maybe I should just keep the cavity. I mean, after all, a cavity is part of your body, too, right? Why should we pick on my tooth just because it's rotting a little bit?"

The dentist smiled, but he said firmly, "Open wide, Alex."

"I don't know," Alex said. "I get a bad feeling about this. Did I ever tell you I was psychic? I don't think this is a good time for drilling."

"Open."

Alex opened wide. The dentist leaned forward, placing the drill in Alex's mouth. Alex closed his eyes. I am famous for my bravery in the dentist's office, he told himself. Want to know how brave I am? Unlike last time, I'm not going to start screaming at the top of my lungs, even before the dentist starts drilling!

Alex felt the drill in his mouth now. The whirring sound

was boring into his brain. The drill bit touched his tooth.

And then an amazing thing happened. The drill sputtered to a halt.

Alex opened his eyes. But the room stayed dark. In the dim light that came through the small window, he saw the dentist staring down at his drill. "Well, Alex, I think you're in luck," said the dentist. "We seem to have blown a fuse."

Alex laughed in happy relief. "You see, Doc," he said. "You should have listened to me!"

The User Friendly computer time-share store on Linden Boulevard was crowded that afternoon. And the room was noisy with the clickety-clack of keyboards as people typed away on the rented computers. Working at the corner machine was a boy in a yellow sweatshirt with a new fade haircut—Jamal Jenkins.

"And on top of everything else, Michael Jordan is modest," typed Jamal. He thought for a moment. "That's just one more reason I think he's the best athlete in the world."

Jamal was typing up his English essay for school. The assignment was to write about your favorite celebrity, saying why you thought he or she was so great. It should have been a fun assignment, but it was turning into a nightmare.

An hour ago, Jamal's home computer had gone dead, just as he typed the last page. He had taken the computer to a repair shop, but they had told him he had lost all his work for good. Not only that, they said they couldn't fix the computer for two weeks!

Jamal stared at the screen. He'd been trying to remember everything he had written last time, but it only came to three pages. He was out of ideas. Why did his computer have to—

Suddenly he had an idea. He could use what had happened to him earlier that afternoon as part of his essay. "While I was writing this paper, my computer broke," he typed. "I was really upset. But then I thought, what would Michael Jordan do in this situation? Even when he's triple-teamed, he still manages to find a way to get to the basket. He never gives up. So I thought, I'll find my way to another computer. What other computer could I use? And then I had the idea to come to this computer store and finish my paper here."

Jamal smiled as he typed on. Writing this part of the story was making him feel a lot better about his broken computer. And the writing was flowing easily now. Before he knew it, he was done. He reached for the save key—

Poof! The screen went black.

So did the lights in the store. All the customers screamed and groaned as one. The store manager, Mr. Chen, hurried out into the street. When he returned, he held up his hand for quiet. "Don't worry," he said. "The lights are off all along the block. Looks like a blackout."

"So why shouldn't we worry?" demanded the large man standing next to Jamal.

"I just lost my novel," cried a woman, pulling on her hair with both hands.

Jamal looked back at his blank screen. He felt like screaming. He rubbed his eyes with his fingertips. Okay, even Michael Jordan loses a game now and then, he told himself. Maybe this just isn't my day.

Anyway, it wouldn't be that hard to rewrite the essay for a third time. His glance fell on his notes. He would just have to—

His notes! They were moving! Ghostwriter was rearranging the letters into a flashing message.

All around him people were yelling. But what Jamal now saw grabbed his attention. In fact, it was as if the people around him had suddenly become totally silent. And with the lights off in the store, the orange glow from Ghostwriter's words looked even brighter.

!SREBBOR !PLEH, flashed the message.

Jamal didn't know why. But as he looked at these strange words, the hairs on the back of his neck stood up.

He had no idea what the message meant. But he knew it was urgent. He ripped off his Ghostwriter pen. He and the team always wore special pens around their necks. Then he started writing as fast as he could. . . .

CHAPTER 3

A GRIG BRACKA IN BRUCKLUH

"This is horrible! Horrible!" moaned the pudgy man in the business suit.

The man was sitting on a subway bench on the downtown D train platform in Manhattan. Sitting next to him was a dark-haired boy in baggy pants and an army jacket—Rob Baker. As usual, Rob had his nose buried in a book.

"I can't believe this," the businessman was saying. "I'm going to lose my client if the train doesn't come this second. I mean, this is crazy! I've been waiting thirty minutes. Hey, I'm talking to you, kid!"

Rob looked up. "Sorry," he said, taken aback. He smiled politely. "I'm sure the train'll come soon."

"Oh, right," said the man angrily.

21

For the first time, Rob looked around the subway platform. He couldn't believe what he was seeing. When he had come down here, he had been one of the only people on the huge platform. Now the place was jam-packed—and still no train in sight.

That was the incredible thing about books. They could take you into a whole other world. He looked at his watch. He'd been waiting forty minutes. He hadn't even noticed the time passing.

The book he was reading was a collection of prize-winning short stories written by teenagers. The Brooklyn Public Library didn't have the book. He had had to come all the way in to the Mid-Manhattan branch to find it. And now he was stuck in Manhattan.

The story he was reading was by a seventeen-year-old named Stuart Kilmer from Madison, Wisconsin. It was about this seventeen-year-old boy in Madison who found himself right in the middle of a huge and dangerous bank robbery. It was exciting, but it was too unrealistic, Rob thought. Things like that never happened in real life.

At least, nothing too exciting had happened to Rob in a while. That is, if you didn't count having a friend like Ghostwriter who sent mysterious messages to you and your other friends!

"*Attention! Attention!*" the subway loudspeakers suddenly blared. "*There's brine a grig bracka in Bruckluh. No drowden suvuh at zis zime!*"

The voice was painfully loud. But static made the announcement impossible to understand. For a moment, the huge crowd on the platform was stunned into silence. Then everyone started yelling in frustration. Not only was there no train. But, as usual, it seemed the loudspeaker system wasn't working either.

"*Attention! Attention!*" the message repeated. "*There's brine a grig bracka in Bruckluh. No drowden suvuh at zis zime!*"

Still sitting, Rob slipped off his neck pen. He pulled out his notepad and started to jot down the words as he had heard them, trying to make sense out of them as best he could.

"ATTENTION! ATTENTION!" he wrote. He paused, saying the next words out loud, trying to guess at their meaning. "THERE'S BEEN A BIG . . ." he wrote. But he was stuck on the next words, BRACKA IN BRUCKLUH.

ATTENTION, READER!
CAN YOU HELP ROB? MY GUESS IS THAT "BRACKA IN BRUCKLUH" HAS SOMETHING TO DO WITH WHAT JUST HAPPENED BACK IN FORT GREENE.
—GHOSTWRITER

23

Rob couldn't make any sense of the message at all. And the loudspeakers kept screeching the words over and over again. People were holding their ears.

Then suddenly the static disappeared and the loudspeaker message came through loud and clear. When the people on the platform heard the words, though, they didn't feel any better.

"Attention! Attention! There's been a big blackout in Brooklyn. No downtown service at this time!"

There were angry shouts. Then the crowd began to surge toward the exits. Rob stood up as well, but he found himself jammed tight in the crowd of angry commuters. He tried to put his pad back in his pocket, but he kept getting pushed to the side. He stepped to the side, but then he was shoved up against the wall.

"Hey!" he said. He said it right into the wall.

Like most of the walls in the station, the part of the wall he was looking at was covered with a beautiful Day-Glo mural by the famous Fort Greene artist Q Martinez. And just then, something started happening on that wall that took Rob's mind off the angry mob scene swarming around him.

The letters in the mural were glowing and swirling. They spun themselves into a new message—

SOMETHING'S UP!—JAMAL

• • •

In the dark studio control booth, Lenni sat with the phone receiver pressed against her ear. On the other end of the line, the phone at her loft was ringing and ringing. She barely noticed the rings. She was busy studying the notepad on her lap.

"Still can't get through to Max?" Fran asked, sticking her head into the room.

Lenni quickly closed her pad. "No, I can't. I'm not even sure if the phone's really ringing. I think the phone lines are all jammed."

"That's probably right," Keith said, joining Fran in the doorway. "I just talked to somebody in the law office next door. They heard on the radio the whole borough of Brooklyn is out. They're telling everybody to get home. Offices are closing. This could be a major disaster."

"C'mon," Fran said to Lenni. "I better take you home."

"Uh . . . great, thanks," Lenni answered. "But can I just try to get through to my dad first?"

As soon as Fran was gone, Lenni reopened her notebook. First there was the strange message from Ghostwriter, !SREBBOR !PLEH. Then a message from Jamal that Ghostwriter had brought her.

THANKS FOR MESSAGE, GHOSTWRITER, wrote Lenni. BUT I CAN'T UNDERSTAND IT. PLEASE HELP.

The letters scrambled. MASS PANIC. WORRIED, answered Ghostwriter.

Lenni shook her head. Her invisible friend could sense danger. Thanks to the blackout, he must be picking up the alarm and fear all over the city. DON'T WORRY, Lenni wrote. THERE'S A BIG BLACKOUT GOING ON.

She looked at what she had written. On second thought, she told herself, maybe Ghostwriter *should* worry. And she should worry too. She wrote, WHERE IS EVERYONE?

Alex had reached the eleventh floor of the Williamsburgh Bank Building. His dentist's office was on the twenty-seventh floor. That meant he had already walked down sixteen flights. This thought made him instantly tired and out of breath. He stopped by the fire door with its blinking red light.

The crowd on the stairs was pushing past him in the dark. "Why are you stopping?" someone snarled at him. "Keep moving!" ordered another voice. But Alex stayed where he was. He looked more closely at the fire door. On every other floor, the message on the fire door read, CAUTION! FIRE DOOR MUST NEVER BE LOCKED. The flashing message on this door now said, BE FOUND. READ!

Alex pulled out his notepad and held it up to the emergency light. Inside were more messages from Ghostwriter and the team. Great. It wasn't enough there was a blackout. It looked as if the team faced some other emergency as well. But he immediately started trying to unscramble !SREBBOR !PLEH.

BORES BE, HLPR! he wrote in his notepad. That didn't help much.

Still standing on the subway platform, Rob was also making guesses at the strange message. "Sir Ebbor, please?" he wondered out loud. A homeless man shuffling past gave him a strange look.

● ATTENTION, READER!
A LITTLE HELP, PLEASE. CAN YOU MAKE SENSE OF THE MESSAGE?
—GHOSTWRITER

At the sound studio, Lenni wrote, I'M STUMPED. GHOST-WRITER, DID YOU FIND ANY OTHER CLUES?

The page stayed blank a long time. Then Ghostwriter started lifting letters all over the page, dancing them into a long reply. NO, SORRY. BUT WHEN I FOUND THE MESSAGE, I SENSED GREAT DISTRESS.

Great, thought Lenni. More pressure. She stared at the message again—

!SREBBOR !PLEH

I give up, she thought.

The moment she gave up, the answer popped into her head.

MORE BAD NEWS

Notepad in hand, Jamal stood outside the computer store, nervously shifting from foot to foot. The rain had come and gone quickly, and the sun was out. That was the good news. The bad news was that the sun was setting.

Mr. Chen, the manager of the store, came outside holding a transistor radio to his ear. "Power's still out all over Brooklyn," he told Jamal. He was looking worried. "Make sure you get home safely!"

"I will," Jamal said. "Thanks." But he stayed where he was as Mr. Chen went back inside. All around Jamal, commuters were arguing over cabs, crowding into buses. But Jamal kept studying his notepad.

Then came a message from Ghostwriter: LENNI'S GOT IT!

Jamal waited tensely. Then the strange message, !SREBBOR !PLEH, began to shake. One after another, the letters flew off the page.

Ghostwriter had written the message backward. It now spelled HELP! ROBBERS!

Yes! thought Jamal. Lenni *had* solved it.

On the subway platform in Manhattan, Rob was thinking the same thing. "Great going, Lenni!" he said aloud. "Now we're getting somewhere." In his notepad, he wrote, GHOST-WRITER, WHY WAS MESSAGE BACKWARD?

I'M CONFUSED, Ghostwriter wrote back.

That makes two of us, thought Rob, nervously running his hand through his dark hair.

In the control booth, Lenni wrote, GHOSTWRITER, PLEASE TRY CHECKING AROUND THE MESSAGE FOR MORE CLUES.

There was a long pause. Then came the message, THIS IS ALL I COULD FIND—QQQQQQQQQQQQQQQQ.

QQQQQQQQQQQQQQQQ? thought Lenni. Maybe some-one's holding their finger down on a computer keyboard. But what computer would be on in a blackout?

"C'mon, guys," Jamal muttered to himself. "We've got to hurry!"

Alex, who was still standing in the dark stairwell of the skyscraper, wrote, GHOSTWRITER, WHERE ARE GABY AND TINA?

I DON'T KNOW. THEY'RE NOT WRITING. I'M WORRIED! was Ghostwriter's upsetting reply.

"Don't worry," Alex told himself, but he started biting his lower lip so hard it hurt. He knew how intense his sister and Tina got when they were doing their video news thing. They probably just kept missing Ghostwriter's messages, he told himself. But he kept biting his lip.

Jamal was studying his notepad, waiting. Finally he wrote, GHOSTWRITER, PLEASE KEEP LOOKING FOR CLUES!

QQQQQQQQQQQQQQQQQQQQQ, Ghostwriter wrote again.

Ghostwriter wrote the same message to Rob on the subway platform in Manhattan. When he saw the message, Rob gasped.

It was such an incredible sight that at first he couldn't make sense of what he was seeing. On both sides of the tracks, the walls were now glowing with purple Qs.

Then he realized what was happening. The walls were covered with murals by Quito Martinez. As Ghostwriter tried to relay his message of Qs, he was lighting up Q's signature all over the place.

Rob gaped at the shiny Qs. Why hadn't he thought of it before?

He started writing so hard his pen ripped through to the next page. I BET THE QS STAND FOR QUITO MARTI-

NEZ, he wrote. AND THAT MEANS—Q'S GETTING ROBBED! GHOSTWRITER—PLEASE SPREAD THE WORD!

He didn't wait for a response. He banged through the turnstile and raced up the stairs two at a time. He needed a pay phone, and fast.

But out on the street, every pay phone was taken, and there were long lines of people waiting. "I need to use the phone," he told an elderly man who was in the middle of dialing. "It's an emergency."

The old man laughed. "You bet it's an emergency. You see all these people?" The old man waved at the crowd. "Everyone is trying to get home. Haven't you heard? Brooklyn is blacked out!"

"But—" Rob started. The man turned away and started his conversation.

Rob ran to the next pay phone, but they wouldn't let him call there either.

Outside the Williamsburgh Bank Building, Alex was running into the same problem. So was Jamal. Only Lenni, who was still in the control booth, had a phone. But everyone in the city must have been calling at once, because she still couldn't get through.

Then finally, on her twentieth try, someone answered at police headquarters.

"I think there's a robbery going on," Lenni said.

"You think?" asked the police officer. She sounded very rushed and angry.

"Yeah," said Lenni quickly. "The artist Q. At his home."

Lenni could hear a lot of yelling going on at the police station. "Look," the officer said, "we'll try to get to this, but in case you haven't heard, we're in the middle of an emergency here." Then she hung up.

"By the way," Gaby whispered to Tina, "did I tell you that I'm afraid of the dark?"

"I'm not too crazy about it either, believe me," Tina whispered back.

The two girls were locked in a room so pitch-dark they couldn't see their hands in front of their faces. Gaby could hear, but not see, Tina moving around. There was a squeaking sound.

"What's *that*?" Gaby gasped. "Mice?"

"No," said Tina. "It's my pen. I'm writing."

"On what?"

"The wall."

"How can you see what you're writing?"

"I can't. But Ghostwriter can."

"Good thinking!" whispered Gaby.

"Thanks."

The squeaking of Tina's pen had stopped. They waited.

"I just thought of something," moaned Gaby. "Even if Ghostwriter writes back to us in here, we won't be able to see his message."

Tina groaned softly. "I didn't think of that."

"Who do you think locked us in here?" Gaby whispered after a moment.

"I don't know," Tina answered. "I didn't get a good look. Someone threw a coat over my head."

"Me too," Gaby said. "Guess there were two of them. Or three—we forgot about Q! I wonder what happened to him."

"I hope he's all right," Tina said slowly.

They were both silent for a while.

"Well, Q said that the museum has night guards," Tina reminded Gaby. "The guards will probably catch these guys, whoever they are."

"And if they don't?"

"Don't worry," Tina replied. "We'll think of something."

Gaby couldn't see her friend's face. In the darkness, all she could do was listen to Tina's voice. And Tina's voice sounded awfully shaky.

"Look at those long lines at Woolworth's," Fran said, pointing.

"Why would everyone go shopping in a blackout?" Lenni wondered.

"Everyone's buying candles," answered another woman on the bus. "Just like the big blackout in 1965."

The bus was packed so tightly, Lenni couldn't turn to see who had spoken. Fran added, "The electronic cash registers must all be out. It must be taking forever to do all those sales."

Lenni and her teammates had decided they would keep calling the police every chance they got, but knew they had better start home. Lenni and Fran the guitarist had climbed down fifteen flights of stairs in the dark. Outside, they joined a huge crowd packing into a bus. The traffic lights were all out, and the bus moved slowly through the dusk.

"Just my luck, I had a date tonight," said another voice in the crowded bus.

"You're in luck," answered another stranger. "Now you'll get to eat by candlelight!"

Everyone laughed. "You see? At least in a blackout, the people of Brooklyn start talking to each other," observed another voice.

The bus stopped again. It seemed to Lenni as if they had gone about three inches in twenty minutes. She was pressed against the rear exit door, facing out the window. Across the street was a newsstand. And on the newspaper rack was a newspaper whose front page was covered with glowing letters.

"I'll be right back," Lenni said as the bus pulled into its next stop.

"Wait!" Fran said. "Where are you going?"

Lenni pointed at the newsstand and kept running.

"You'll never make it! Come back!"

Lenni turned and jogged in place long enough to shout back, "The bus isn't going anywhere. I'll be right there!"

She raced to the newsstand and grabbed the paper. But a large fist closed over her hand.

"Fifty cents," demanded the man in the booth.

Lenni dug in her pocket, but her jeans were tight and she couldn't squeeze her fingers inside. She glanced back in a panic. The bus was pulling out. Jammed inside, Fran was waving at her frantically.

Sure, Lenni thought, *now* the traffic clears.

She got her hand in her pocket and yanked out the change, but it flew all over the street. And by the time she had picked up the coins and paid for the paper, the bus was gone. She tried to run after it, but the masses of people walking home blocked the sidewalk.

Lenni moved out of the way of the crowd and studied the flashing letters on the paper's front page.

H	F	Y	O	U	C	A	N	R	E
A	E	T	H	I	S	S	I	G	N
T	H	L	N	I	M	U	S	T	S
A	Y	Y	P	U	C	A	N	S	E
E	T	H	E	!	A	I	N	I	N
T	H	E	H	O	–	D	Y	O	H
E	R	E	S	T	H	G	M	O	S
T	P	A	I	N	F	U	&	T	H
I	N	G	O	F	A	L	L	T	E
S	H	A	R	E	T	H	E	B	L

GHOSTWRITER? Lenni wrote in her notepad. WHAT'S THIS?

ALEX SUGGESTED I CHECK AROUND TINA AND GABY FOR CLUES, Ghostwriter wrote back.

AND YOU FOUND ALL THESE LETTERS? WHAT DOES IT MEAN?

I DON'T HAVE A CLUE, Ghostwriter answered. BUT I FEAR THAT TIME IS RUNNING OUT.

Ghostwriter passed along the strange mass of letters to the rest of the team.

Maybe it's code, thought Rob, who was still stranded on a street in Manhattan, waiting for a phone.

Maybe Gaby's using a broken typewriter, thought Alex, who was standing outside the Williamsburgh Bank Building.

The message seems to read from left to right, thought Jamal as he studied his notepad outside the computer store. He carefully rewrote the letters in long lines.

H F Y O U C A N R E A E T H I S S I G N T H L N I
M U S T S A Y Y P U C A N S E E T H E ! A I N I N T H
E H O–D Y O H E R E S T H G M O S T P A I N F U & T
H I N G O F A L L T E S H A R E T H E B L.

As he stared at the long string of letters, he started to make out some words. He started adding slash marks as he tried to break the message down into words.

H F/ Y O U/ C A N/ R E A E/ T H I S/ S I G N/ T H L N/
I/ M U S T/ S A Y/ Y P U/ C A N/ S E E/ T H E/ ! A I N/
I N/ T H E/ H O–D/ Y O/ H E R E S/ T H G/ M O S T/
P A I N F U &/ T H I N G/ O F/ A L L/ T E/ S H A R E/
T H E/ B L.

Suddenly the letters lifted off the page. Ghostwriter was transporting Jamal's work to his teammates!

When he got the message, Alex immediately saw what his teammate Jamal was up to. He tried to say the message out loud, guessing at the mixed-up words. HF could be IF. REAE could be READ. Then the message would start IF YOU CAN READ THIS SIGN . . .

Working this way, he was able to guess at all the wrong letters in the message. He quickly wrote, H=I, E=D, L=E, P=O, !=P, -=O, G =E, &=L, T=W.

Now he wrote out the decoded message. IF YOU CAN READ THIS SIGN, THEN I MUST SAY YOU CAN SEE THE PAIN IN THE HOOD. YO, HERE'S THE MOST PAINFUL THING OF ALL: WE SHARE THE BL

GHOSTWRITER, he added. PLEASE PASS THIS ON!

When Rob got the decoded message, he thought about the graffiti he had seen down in the subway. It sounded like one of Q's paintings. Then he realized something else. The wrong letters in the message were all in a row. They were on a diagonal from top to bottom. He went back to the original block of letters and started to draw a loop around the wrong letters.

🔔 ATTENTION, READER!
CAN YOU FIND THE HIDDEN MESSAGE?
  —GHOSTWRITER

Ghostwriter passed along Rob's answer to Lenni and Alex and Jamal.

HELP—G&T!

Immediately the teammates all started writing at once. Everyone was asking, WHERE ARE YOU, GABY AND TINA?

Spread out all over the darkening city, Alex, Lenni, Rob, and Jamal waited for an answer from their missing teammates.

They waited and waited. The only message they got was a message that Ghostwriter brought from Rob. SOUNDS LIKE THEY'RE WRITING OVER A Q PAINTING, Rob wrote.

When he saw these words form in his notepad, Alex gave a shout. Of course! Gaby and Tina were interviewing Q today for their video project. And that meant they were mixed up in this robbery!

I'M GOING TO TRY TO FIND A POLICE OFFICER, Alex wrote back at once.

WAIT! came the message from Ghostwriter. ROB WRITES THAT POLICE ARE TOO BUSY WITH BLACKOUT.

Alex ran to the nearest phone anyway, dialing 911. It took six tries before he got through. And as Rob had predicted, the police were way too busy with a million other emergencies to pay any attention to Alex.

OKAY. WE HAVE NO CHOICE! Alex wrote in his notepad in big bold letters. IT'S UP TO US. WE'VE GOT TO GET TO Q'S APARTMENT RIGHT AWAY. I FOUND A PHONE BOOK. He wrote down Q's address for the whole group.

Outside the newsstand, Lenni memorized the address. SEE YOU AT Q'S APARTMENT, she wrote. Then she clapped her notepad shut. So did Jamal back at the computer store and Rob in Manhattan. No one waited long enough to catch Ghostwriter's message: TAKE CARE, MY CHILDREN!

Outside the bank building, Alex started dodging his way

through the crowds of pedestrians. His heart was pounding. He tried to calm himself down by reviewing what they had to do.

That didn't help at all. Somehow they had to make it through a blackout to Q's apartment and stop the burglars all by themselves!

Even though he kept bumping into people, Alex started to run. He glanced up at the sky.

More bad news, he realized. Darkness was falling fast.

CHAPTER 5

RACING IN THE DARK

The blacked-out street was snarled with cabs, cars, buses, fire trucks, ambulances, and other emergency vehicles. The sky had now turned as dark as the streetlights. Yellow headlights and flashing red lights were the only lights Jamal saw.

He felt as if he had hailed about six hundred cabs. Finally he got one to stop.

"Three forty-nine Lafayette," he told the driver. "The Bradley Warehouse. And please hurry!"

"That's a laugh," said the driver, but he didn't laugh. "Look at this traffic." He held his hand out. "Fifty dollars."

"What?!"

"You heard me. Fifty. And I want it up front."

"But that's against the law," Jamal said. "You have to go by what the meter says."

The cabdriver pointed out at the darkness. "Take a look around, kid. No meter tonight," he said. "Fifty dollars. Take it or leave it."

"I only have six on me," Jamal said, checking his wallet.

The cabdriver worked his cab back over to the curb. The lock on the door next to Jamal clicked open. "See ya," the driver said.

Meanwhile, over on Tillary Street, Alex was running as fast as he could. Which was not fast at all. As in a nightmare, the crowds on the sidewalks seemed to be getting thicker and thicker, as if the whole world were headed home. Everyone but the Ghostwriter team. Everyone but Gaby and Tina.

"Flashlights! Flashlights! Get your flashlights for the black-out!" a vendor was yelling.

Alex rushed up to him. "How much?"

"Three," said the salesman.

Alex peered at the cheesy plastic flashlights the man was selling. Three dollars was a rip-off, but he didn't have time to bargain. He found the money in his wallet and handed it over. Then he clicked the flashlight on. Nothing happened.

"Plus two dollars more for batteries," said the vendor with a mean grin.

Lenni, meanwhile, had managed to jam her way onto another bus. There were people standing out in the middle of most of the street crossings now. They were ordinary people from the neighborhood who were trying to pitch in and help direct the traffic through the dark. They were taking a big risk, Lenni realized, standing out there in the dark. And she felt a swell of admiration.

But even with all the volunteers helping, Lenni's bus was moving very slowly.

"C'mon, c'mon," Lenni urged.

"In a hurry?" asked the amused old woman standing next to her. "The best thing to do in one of these crises is just relax. If you give up worrying about being late, you could even have a good time."

Lenni tried to smile. "Thanks," she said. But what she was thinking was, There's no way Gaby and Tina are having a good time right now.

Someone tapped her shoulder. It was the old woman. "I bought an extra flashlight," she said, holding the small plastic torch toward Lenni.

"Oh, wow, that's so nice of you," Lenni exclaimed. "But I couldn't take it."

The old woman pressed the flashlight into her hand. "Nonsense. This is an emergency. You take it."

Lenni smiled gratefully. "Thanks."

It was at the same moment that Rob reached the middle of the Brooklyn Bridge.

The bridge was a solid mass of people—like the pictures Rob had seen in the papers during the New York City Marathon. Everyone was walking through the darkness, over the bridge and back from Manhattan. Up ahead, Brooklyn's skyline looked eerily dark.

It made Rob feel a lot better to see several police scooters cruising slowly forward along with the crowd. But there was no way he could get close enough to the officers to ask for help. Rob kept working his way forward, going as fast as possible.

"Look," said a woman next to him in the dark. She pointed up. Now that Brooklyn was blacked out, he could see thousands of stars twinkling overhead.

"I didn't know they had stars over New York!" Rob said.

The woman laughed. "Me neither!"

Alex hurried down Lafayette Avenue. Almost all the windows of the apartments now had lit candles in them, like one huge jack-o'-lantern. It was a strange and beautiful sight, but Alex had no time to appreciate it. Please, please, please let them be okay, he prayed.

Out of the whole group, he had started out closest to the Bradley Warehouse. He got there first. The huge square building had once been used to make buttons. Bradley Managers of Apartments had turned the place into loft apartments. The rundown ten-story building rose before him in the darkness. It looked scary and evil. Gaby! He ran forward.

In the dark lobby, Alex found chaos, with police officers and firefighters rushing in and out.

"I think there's a robbery going on on the tenth floor," he shouted at the first man he could find.

"You think?" the man said, rushing past him. "Because I *know* we've got a pregnant woman stuck in the freight elevator on the sixth floor!"

The man was gone, vanishing into the darkness. Alex tried to grab the attention of a few more people, but they were moving too fast, shouting orders at one another, pushing him out of the way. Then his flashlight beam caught the red letters on a door marked STAIRS. He yanked open the door.

He paused. At least in the lobby there was a little light spilling in from the emergency vehicles outside. The stairwell was pitch-dark. He didn't pause long. He started up the stairs two at a time.

His flashlight jiggled wildly as he ran. It shone on the strange faces of people and animals that lined the stairs. Q had decorated the stairwell with eerie Day-Glo murals.

"Help! Help!" a woman's voice moaned.

Alex came to an abrupt halt.

"Hang in there, we're coming," shouted another voice.

Then he realized what he was hearing. He must be near the elevator shaft where the people were trapped. That meant he was on the sixth floor.

Hang in there, Gaby and Tina! he yelled to himself. I'm coming!

Then he turned the corner and nearly fainted. A huge man with the claws of a lion leaped out at him.

But it was only another of Q's drawings.

Finally he made it to the tenth floor. The hallway was dark and silent. His footsteps echoed on the bare wood floor. He shone his light on a metal door. 10-A.

Then he found 10-B. But he didn't need the door number to know he had come to the right place. Spray-painted across the door was a large purple Q.

Now what? he wondered. The door was closed. Should he ring the bell?

If there were burglars in there, they wouldn't be likely to answer the door. What would they say? Sorry, we can't talk to you right now, we're busy robbing this apartment!

Alex was still gasping from the stairs. But now his heart started pounding even faster than before. He put his hand on the doorknob—and turned it.

Suddenly, from behind him, a voice growled, "Make one more move and I'll shoot."

CHAPTER 6

"HE'S DEAD!"

Alex froze. I think I fainted, he told himself. His hands rose as if by themselves, and his flashlight was now pointing straight up at the ceiling.

"Turn around real slow," the voice instructed him.

He turned around, ready to face the robber. In the dark hallway, he could barely make out who he was looking at. It was a tall African American woman, that much he could see. She was holding something, something wooden—a baseball bat.

"Now just what do you think you're doing?" the woman demanded.

"I—I—"

"You thought because we're having a blackout that you could do some looting, huh?"

"No! Listen!" Alex lowered his voice. "I think there's a robbery going on in there. And my sister—we got an urgent message—"

The words were tumbling out. The woman lowered the baseball bat. "Okay, okay," she said. "Hold on. I've got spare keys to Q's apartment; we'll take a look."

She stepped back into the darkness. A door opened and shut. Alex waited. He couldn't hear any sound coming from Q's apartment. The silence was scary.

Then Q's neighbor was back. "My name's Glorious, by the way," she whispered to him as she fumbled with a set of keys. "Glorious Johnson."

"Alex Fernandez."

"Q hasn't been back here all this afternoon," she said. "I know that. I kind of watch his place for him when he's gone. So I don't see how—"

She unlocked the door and let it swing open. They both stood in front of the doorway, staring into the darkness. Alex tensed, as if something might spring out at him. There was only more darkness, more silence.

"Hold on," Glorious said. A match flared. She was lighting a candle. Then she picked up the baseball bat with her other hand. "Okay," she said. "Let's go."

They entered the apartment. Alex shone his flashlight around in wide arcs. He caught glimpses of canvas after canvas of spray-painted art. The big, echoing space was messy, but other than that, nothing seemed to have been disturbed. The loft appeared to be empty.

"Q?" Glorious called.

"Gaby? Tina?" said Alex. Then he turned.

Glorious's face was lit by her candle. She looked very creepy with the light shining up at her like that. "There was no robbery here," she said. "What kind of story are you making up?"

"It's no story! I'm telling you, my sister—"

"Your sister. You probably don't even have a sister. You're a pretty smooth talker, though. I'll give you that much. But now you'd better start smooth-talking yourself right out of this apartment."

By the light of the candle, Alex could see her raising the bat again. That was all he needed. "Q's in trouble," he said, backing out of the room. "I just don't know where. You don't have any idea where he might be, do you?"

Glorious was marching slowly after him as he backed up. Alex knocked into something in the darkness—a lamp?—and it fell with a crash.

Alex turned and ran as fast as he could, ducking out the open front door. He raced back down the hallway, banging open the metal door to the stairwell. He took the stairs three at a time.

Then he turned the corner.

And ran smack into someone coming the other way.

He screamed. Whoever it was, they both fell, their flashlights bouncing away down the steps. That left them in total darkness.

Alex tried to scramble back to his feet, but the person grabbed him. "Wait!" cried a familiar voice. "Alex! It's me!"

"Lenni! Am I glad to see—" But then he remembered Q's neighbor. "C'mon!"

He grabbed Lenni's hand and led her back down the stairs. They scooped up their flashlights and kept on running.

It wasn't until they were outside the building that Alex finally stopped to explain.

"So if they're not at his apartment, then where are they?" Lenni said.

"I don't know."

They stared at each other. Alex looked so desperate that Lenni joked, "I guess we're in the dark."

But Alex was in no mood for humor. He started hurrying on down the street. "Alex," Lenni said. "Where are you going? We don't know where they are."

Alex stopped and faced her. He banged his fists against his legs. She was right. "What a time for a blackout," he said. He looked up at the star-filled sky. "Turn the power back on!" he yelled.

As if in answer to his command, a jagged streak of lightning cracked through the sky. The lightning lit up the street, but only for a second, as if to tease them. Then came the thunder, and then the rain started again.

"Nice going," Lenni said. "You got what you wished for. Look, we have to let Rob and Jamal know what's up." She took out her notepad. Alex shone his flashlight on the page for her.

Q WASN'T THERE, Lenni started to write. But the rain made the ink run before she could even get the words down.

"Oh, great," Alex said miserably.

"Alex," Lenni said. "Maybe we should go back to our first plan."

"What was that?"

"Try to get home and find our parents. They're going to be worried sick about all of us."

Alex shook his head. "They're going to be even more worried when they hear about Tina and Gaby. There isn't time, Lenni. C'mon." Pulling his windbreaker up over his head as a hood, he started running down the street. Lenni followed him as he ducked into a bus shelter. "We can write in here," Alex said. "Shine your light so I can see."

Lenni shone her flashlight across the walls of the bus shelter, which were covered with flyers advertising cheap moving vans, apartment sales, sublets, cleaning services. Writing as quickly as he could on one of the flyers, Alex asked Ghostwriter to read everything he could find near Gaby and Tina.

The flyer he was writing on read, MOVING SALE, EVERY-THING MUST GO! Only now the letters were moving, re-arranging. Ghostwriter pulled out four letters. GLEN.

"Glen?" Alex wondered out loud.

The letters spun again.

STU.

"Glen and Stu?" Lenni said softly. "Never heard of them."

"This is getting us nowhere," Alex said.

"Maybe they're the robbers," Lenni said.

"So?" Alex said. "What are we going to do? Try to call the cops and tell them the robbers' first names?"

The letters moved one last time. RELEASE T, G!

"Release Tina and Gaby," read Alex. "We're trying, Ghost-writer. We're trying!"

Alex shone his light around the booth, looking for more messages. "C'mon, c'mon," he growled. But no new messages appeared.

"I'm going to try to call the police again," Lenni said. "Where are we?" She peered out into the rain, looking for a street sign. She found one. They were at the intersection of CUMBERLAND and HANSON.

Alex shone his light out of the bus stop. "BMOA?" he said.

"Huh? No, it's Hanson," Lenni corrected him, starting to run. But Alex grabbed her arm, holding her back. "No, look!"

She followed the beam of his flashlight back to the street

sign. Ghostwriter had changed the letters, spelling out BMOA.

"Great," moaned Alex. He knew Ghostwriter was trying his best. But this was another clue that seemed to make no sense.

"A mob?" wondered Lenni, turning the letters around in her head.

"A mob," repeated Alex, thinking this over. "We've seen plenty of those tonight. With everyone trying to get home before it got dark, there were mobs everywhere."

"Not anymore," Lenni said. She gestured with her flashlight at the dark, rainy street. Only a few pedestrians were still making their way home.

"BMOA, BMOA," Alex said, starting to pace inside the bus stop.

"Best Monday of All?" guessed Lenni.

"That's a laugh," Alex grumbled. Then he stopped and stared at her.

"Alex, don't shine your light in my eyes."

"But Lenni," he said eagerly. "I think you're right. It's initials."

"Beautiful Makers of Autos?" Lenni guessed.

"Best Movers of America?" answered Alex.

Now they were both pacing, shouting out guesses. "B," said Alex. "Baker, barber, beauty shop—"

"Bob, Bill, Brad—"

Alex snapped his fingers. "Brad!"

"You know a Brad?" Lenni asked.

"No," admitted Alex. "But that name rings a bell for some reason. Brad, Brad, Bradley!" He shouted out the last name.

"Bradley Managers," breathed Lenni.

"Bradley Managers of," said Alex.

They finished the phrase together. "Apartments."

They both said the letters again. "BMOA!"

Then they started to run.

Jamal was still on foot. He was trying to track his route by following the tall, pointed spire of the Cooper Building, which he knew was near the Bradley Warehouse. GLEN, STU, GLEN, STU, BMOA—he repeated Ghostwriter's clues over and over. He couldn't make any sense out of them. Then he reached the Cooper Building. Only it wasn't the Cooper Building at all. It was the Rodgers Armory, which also had a spire.

"No!" he gasped. But he knew there was nothing he could say or do that would change what had happened. He had just gone fifteen blocks in the wrong direction.

Lester Bradley was one of the biggest managers of apartments in Fort Greene. Q had done a lot of his mural work for Bradley buildings. It made perfect sense.

It took Lenni and Alex only ten minutes to reach the Bradley building. But it took them another twenty minutes to climb the stairs to the twenty-fourth floor.

"When this is all over, I'm going to start a stair-climbing team at Hurston," Alex panted.

Lenni was glad to hear Alex making jokes again. But she was too tired to laugh.

At last they made it to the twenty-fourth floor. Shining their flashlights ahead of them, the two friends made their way down a hallway lined with pebbly glass office doors. Suddenly Alex stopped short. He thought he had heard someone. It took him a moment to realize that the strange sound was their ragged gasps for air. They were both exhausted.

Finally they found the office labeled BRADLEY MANAGERS. There was no sound coming from inside.

Lenni and Alex exchanged glances. Then Alex shone his light on the doorknob. Lenni nodded slightly. Alex turned the knob. It was open. They went in.

As far as they could tell by the beams of two small flashlights, the office was neat and deserted. Plastic dust covers had been put back on computers and typewriters. Everyone had gone home.

They came to a hallway. Alex went left. Lenni went right. She checked all the offices she passed. No one here.

Then she came to the last office, which looked as if it must be Mr. Bradley's. With its walnut paneling, this room seemed even darker than the rest. But just as empty.

Then a hand dropped onto her shoulder.

Lenni jumped straight up into the air. "Sorry," Alex whispered. "Listen, I checked all the rooms. Nobody's here. Looks like another dead end."

Sighing, Lenni let her hand—the hand with the flashlight—fall to her side. Then she looked at what the flashlight was now pointing to. A human hand.

She jerked her flashlight forward, revealing the rest of the body, which was lying facedown on the rug.

"Oh no! It must be Q," she whispered. "Alex—he's dead!"

CHAPTER 7

B IS FOR BROOKLYN

"Q!" yelled Alex. He dropped to his feet and shook the body.

The body turned over and looked up at them, blinking in the light of their flashlights. The body was not dead, and it was not Q.

"Who are you?" gasped Lenni.

The old man started to get to his feet. "Who am I? I'm Lester Bradley, the owner of this company. Who are *you*? And what are you doing in my office?"

"We're l-looking for Q," Alex stammered as he and Lenni backed away.

The man groaned and stretched. He was mostly bald with a fringe of gray hair, Lenni now saw. How could she have thought this was Q!

"Looking for Q?" Mr. Bradley said. He seemed bewildered.

"Quito Martinez," explained Lenni, backing up even farther. "We thought he might be here—"

"We thought he might be in trouble," Alex added.

"I haven't seen Q in weeks," said the man. "I have no idea where he is." The man groaned again. "Oof—I'm too old to be sleeping on the floor. But I'm also too old to climb down twenty-four flights and walk home. I take it they don't have the power back on yet?"

"No," Lenni said. "They don't." She had reached the doorway now.

"Now what's this about Q in trouble?" Mr. Bradley demanded.

Lenni and Alex were backing out the door. "Nothing," Alex called back into the dark office. "We're sorry to bother you."

"You kids shouldn't be running around in the middle of a blackout," he called after them. "Go home."

"We will," Lenni promised. As tired as they were, they didn't stop running until they had reached the landing of the twentieth floor.

"What are you looking for?" Tina asked in the darkness.

"I don't know," Gaby said. "But maybe there's something in this room that will help us escape." She was moving slowly through the pitch-dark room, swinging her arms slowly from side to side. Her foot hit something. She knelt down and felt with her hands. Then she jumped back and started screaming.

What she had felt was a human head.

"Tina, there's someone in here," Gaby cried when she was able to stop screaming. "I think he's dead!"

"Oh no!" Tina exclaimed. Gaby was back at her side, clutching her arm. Both girls were screaming now.

Suddenly Tina stopped. "Let go," she said, shaking Gaby's hand away. "I've got an idea."

"What? What? What?"

"We're so stupid. We should write where we are, that we're in the museum."

Just then, there was the sound of footsteps running down the hallway. The lock turned and the door was flung open. A big, dark shape filled the doorway and a powerful flashlight shone into Gaby's eyes. Then it swept to the other side of the room. In its light, Gaby could see the body—the bodies—on the floor. Three museum guards—all unconscious.

Thanks to Q, she and Tina had been able to stay in the museum after closing hours. Now she knew why there hadn't been any night guards around to protect them from the bad guys, whoever they were.

In the same split second, she saw something else. Every inch of the room's walls was covered with one of Q's murals. They'd written their first message right over Q's painting!

"Who screamed?" demanded a deep voice from the doorway. Gaby and Tina were shaking too hard to answer.

"Hey!" snapped a squeaky voice. A little, skinny shadow darted over and grabbed the pen out of Tina's hand. He snatched Gaby's as well.

"Try screaming again," warned the big shadow, "and it'll be the last sound you make." Then both men backed out and slammed the door, returning the girls to pitch-darkness.

"I don't know what kind of crazy scheme you kids have working," Glorious Johnson told Jamal. "But your friend was already here and we already checked the place. Q's not home and there was no robbery."

Jamal and Glorious were standing in the dark hallway outside Q's apartment. Jamal was just beginning to get his breath back from the scare of seeing the woman with the baseball bat. "My friend was here?" he asked. "Which one?"

"You tell me," Glorious said. "How many of you are there running around tonight anyway?"

"What did he look like?" Jamal asked patiently.

"About your height, dark eyes, handsome—I didn't get that good a look at him because of the dark." She shone her flashlight in Jamal's face. "But if you kids are up to something, I'll remember what you look like, believe me."

"Thanks," Jamal said, edging around her and heading for the stairwell. So Alex had already been here. Why hadn't he signaled Jamal that Q *wasn't* here?

Out on the street, he started writing in his notepad. RA was as far as he got. His pen, wet with the rain, had now run out of ink.

Just like I told you before, it's not your day, Jamal said to himself. He started down the street in the rain, studying his notes by the light of the small flashlight he'd bought.

Glen. Stu. Glen. Stu. Drops of rain spattered the page. A drop hit the name Glen square on, making the letters run.

BMOA. The rain soon washed away these letters as well.

Now I'm really out of clues, Jamal thought. He started running again, just to feel as if he was doing *something*. He passed a man carrying a transistor.

"Any news?" Jamal asked him.

"All of Brooklyn is still out," the man told him. "They're asking people to unplug all appliances."

"Thanks." Jamal ran on—as if he had someplace to run to!

Brooklyn, Jamal thought.

Then he stopped short and studied his notepad. The words he had written were now only blotches of pale green. But he was picturing the letters BMOA in his mind. Brooklyn. What if the first letter, B, stood for Brooklyn?

● ATTENTION, READER!
I BELIEVE JAMAL IS RIGHT. THE FIRST LET-
TER OF BMOA DOES STAND FOR BROOKLYN.
ALSO, I THINK THE FOUR INITIALS STAND FOR
A PLACE ALREADY MENTIONED IN THIS BOOK!
PLEASE FIGURE IT OUT!
    —GHOSTWRITER

"Brooklyn, Brooklyn, Brooklyn," muttered Jamal as he walked down the street. Suddenly the rest of the phrase fell into his head. The phrase clicked into his mind like the missing piece in a jigsaw puzzle.

The Brooklyn Museum of Art. Q had a show at the museum right now. What if Gaby and Tina had gone there to interview Q for their video news report?

He was running faster now, but he stopped running almost immediately. Finding a pebble, he scratched out a message on the sidewalk. BMOA = BROOKLYN MUSEUM OF ART.

Only three blocks away, Rob was jogging through the rain. Running in the dark with no flashlight, he missed the messages that appeared on the street signs he passed.

At the same time, Lenni and Alex were making their way down the endless steps of the Bradley building. "We'd better turn off our flashlights and save the batteries," Alex suggested.

They clicked off their flashlights—just as Jamal's message appeared on the fire extinguisher mounted on the wall above them.

Back on the sidewalk, Jamal stood in the rain, staring down at his message. Pedestrians were walking past him now, stepping on the letters, helping the rain smooth the message away.

His teammates would have the message by now, anyway, he thought. They would meet him at the museum.

Glad that he wasn't in this alone, he started to run.

CHAPTER 8

THE UNDERGROUND

Alex and Lenni were hurrying down Market Street, past a wooden wall around a huge construction site. Lenni stopped. "Wait!"

Alex started jogging in place. "What?"

"Nothing . . . it's just . . . I think I'm having a heart attack."

Waiting, Alex leaned against the wooden wall, which was covered with posters.

"Lenni," Alex said quietly, when he had gotten his breath back. "I'm really scared."

"I know," Lenni said. She was looking down, drawing deep breaths. Now she looked up. Her eyes widened. "Alex—" she said. She started pointing.

Alex whirled. The posters he had been leaning on were all identical. They all showed a swirly spray-painted figure that

69

was half-man, half-dragon. In the corner was a purple Q. At the bottom, the poster said BROOKLYN MUSEUM OF ART, January 2–January 29, 1994.

"So?" Alex said.

"BMOA!" shouted Lenni.

Alex looked back at the poster, and then they started running again. "Wait!" Lenni yelled once more. On the sidewalk she began hastily writing with a pebble, BMOA =

About twenty blocks away, Rob was in a phone booth, trying one more time to get through to the police and his parents. The endless busy signal buzzed in his ears. He was about to hang up the phone when he saw the cover of his book of short stories. Four of the letters in the title were flashing. BMOA. He opened the cover to the first page and watched the rest of the message appear. Brooklyn Museum of Art. He slammed the book shut and backed out of the phone booth in a hurry.

Like everything else in the neighborhood at this moment, the Brooklyn Museum of Art was dark. But Jamal was still sure he had come to the right place. The building looked too quiet somehow.

He was still about a half block away from the large museum when he saw it. On a skylight on the side of the building, someone had spray-painted the Day-Glo message !SREBBOR !PLEH.

The message must have been written by someone *inside* the

museum. Whoever it was, they had tried to write so someone outside could read the message and had reversed the letters. But they had forgotten to reverse the order as well. Must have been in a terrible hurry.

Though his sides were aching, Jamal started running again.

Right outside the museum, three Con Ed trucks were parked near an open manhole. Set up around the manhole were several yellow CAUTION, MEN WORKING signs. Jamal paused outside the manhole. There must be workers down there, workers who could help him. After all, he wasn't going to have much luck against a bunch of robbers all by himself. On the other hand, the thought of climbing down into that dark manhole was kind of creepy.

Just then a door slammed. A big, burly Con Ed worker was coming out of one of the trucks, followed by a little Con Ed worker. Jamal ran toward them.

"There's a robbery going on inside the museum," Jamal blurted out.

The Con Ed men looked very surprised. "Huh?" asked the big one.

"What makes you say that?" asked the little man. He had a high-pitched voice.

"Uh . . ." Jamal stammered for an answer. He couldn't exactly say that he'd heard of it from a ghost. "There's a message painted on the window over there. It says, 'Help! Robbers!' "

The big man smiled nervously. " 'Help! Robbers!'? That's—that's—"

"That's a joke," answered the little man.

"Right," said the big man. "It's a Halloween prank."

"Halloween?" Jamal said. "It's January."

"Look, kid"—the little man started past Jamal—"we're very busy right now trying to get the power back on. If you don't mind—"

Jamal grabbed the big man's arm. At least he tried to. The man was too big and strong, his arm too thick. "Please," Jamal said, raising his voice. "I can't tell you how I know for sure, but I know, okay? I know. There are robbers in there and two of my friends are trapped in there too. If you don't help me I'll get the police—"

"Whoa, whoa, whoa." The big man had Jamal by the arm now. He was squeezing tight. "Here, come with us." He was leading Jamal toward the manhole.

"What are you doing?" Jamal asked.

"We've got phone lines working down here," the shorter Con Ed man said. "We can get you through to the police and you can explain the whole story."

Jamal was surprised. Why did the men suddenly believe his story? "Thanks," Jamal said. He didn't like the way the big Con Ed man was pushing him, but if he could get a call through to the police—

Now he was climbing down into the open hole, placing his sneakers carefully on the rungs of the metal ladder. The large Con Ed man shone his flashlight for him. Jamal looked up. The two men smiled at him. "That's it," the little man said. "Go on."

They both followed him. The big man grunted painfully as he squeezed through the hole. "After you," he told Jamal when they were both standing in the underground tunnel.

Jamal walked on ahead of the two Con Ed workers. Why did he feel as if he was being marched somewhere like a prisoner?

"We think the whole blackout started here," the little Con Ed man said from behind him. "See, this is one of the city's many power centers. Someone cut the feed to the museum."

Jamal stopped and turned. "Cut the what?"

"The feed. That's the line that carries electricity to a building from the street's main cable. Every building has to be hooked up to a main electrical cable that carries the power for several city blocks."

"The thieves did it," Jamal said suddenly.

"Huh?"

"They probably wanted to knock out the museum's security systems or something."

The big man scratched his chin. "You might be right. We've been trying to figure out why anyone would have done this."

The big man prodded Jamal with his flashlight. Jamal turned the corner into a large room filled with electrical equipment and wiring. The room was silent and dark and smelled of smoke.

"Smells like a fire," Jamal said nervously.

"Yup," said the little man. "When they cut the feed wire, there was a short circuit. That started a fire and knocked out the whole room. And then the rest of Brooklyn must have blacked out in a chain reaction."

"Okay, okay," the big man said, slapping the little man on the back. "He doesn't need a whole lecture."

"Uh, the phone," Jamal urged.

"Oh, right," said the big man casually.

Suddenly Jamal realized what had been nagging at him all this time. If the Con Ed men thought the blackout had started here, shouldn't they be hard at work trying to get the power center going again? Shouldn't there be *more* workers down here right now?

He turned back toward the big Con Ed worker. The burly man was looking back at Jamal with a strange glint in his eye.

Then Jamal saw it. Ghostwriter was making something flash on the men's uniforms. Their name tags.

GLEN.

STU.

CHAPTER 9

A MUSEUM TOUR

There was about a foot of space in between the big man and the small man. Jamal raced toward the space the way he did in football when he snaked through a line of tacklers.

But Glen moved one step to his left, closing the hole. Jamal banged into the burly man's huge stomach and bounced backward. He fell against a control panel.

"You're not going anywhere," Glen said with a smile.

"You know," Stu told Jamal, "when we found out we had caused the blackout, we thought our boss, Violet, would be really mad. But she wasn't. You want to know why?"

Jamal didn't answer. He wasn't listening. He was desperately trying to think of a way out.

"She wasn't mad because a disaster like this means that every available police officer and fire fighter is busy tonight. And you know what that means, don't you?"

Glen was looking confused. "Hey, what *does* that mean?"

Stu rolled his eyes. "That means that no one is going to find *him* until we're gone." He pointed at Jamal.

"Oh, right. Long gone," added Glen.

Then the two men backed out of the door at the same time, bumping into each other. Stu grunted in pain. Then he closed the door. Jamal heard a nasty little click as the door locked.

Alex and Lenni turned the corner onto Eastern Parkway. The traffic lights were all still out. But at least the rain had stopped again, and now the moon was rising overhead.

"There!" Lenni pointed at the large building with the white columns. The place looked deserted. They ran across the wide, deserted street.

Lenni reached the large front doors first. She shone her flashlight on a sticker just next to the door. WARNING—THESE PREMISES ARE GUARDED BY EAGLE EYE ELEC-TRONIC SECURITY SYSTEMS.

Alex shrugged. He pushed the door handle. The metal and glass doors clicked harmlessly, opening inward. They went in.

They entered a huge dark lobby. Large arches led in two directions. They both went left, moving as quickly and quietly as they could.

Lenni stopped and put her hand out to stop Alex as well. "Look," she whispered.

He followed the beam of her flashlight. "I don't see a thing," he whispered back.

"Exactly."

"Huh?"

"The walls are *bare*."

"Q's paintings are gone," Alex said, with a sickening feeling in his stomach. Looking more closely, they could now see the hooks on which the huge canvases had recently hung. They hurried onward.

They ran through three more big rooms before they came to a dead end.

"Ow!" groaned Alex. He had skinned his knee on a stone bench in the middle of the room. "I think we're too late," he said, his voice shaky. "They've taken everything. They wouldn't stick around after they cleaned the place out." He opened his mouth, about to shout out his sister's name. But Lenni clapped her hand over his mouth, muffling the sound. She beamed her flashlight slowly around the walls.

Alex saw what she was showing him. The room was lined with huge, colorful paintings by Q. "I think the robbers are still here," she whispered.

Alex jumped to his feet. "Listen!" he hissed.

Lenni listened. At first she thought her ears might be playing tricks on her. No. The sounds were distant, but they were real. And they were coming this way.

"He knew about the whole operation," said a high-pitched man's voice.

"He knew more than I knew," said a deep voice.

"Please, Violet," said the high voice.

At the mention of the woman's name, Alex and Lenni turned and glanced at each other in the dark.

"We've filled up two out of three trucks," the high voice went on. "Let's not push our luck."

"No," said an icy woman's voice. "I want it all."

Lenni and Alex began frantically beaming their lights around the room, looking for an exit. The stone benches were solid. No place to hide underneath them. Alex pulled on Lenni's hand. He led her into the farthest corner. They pressed themselves back up against the wall. Lenni clicked off her flashlight. Alex clicked off his as well. Except his light stayed on.

"What's some little punk going to do, anyway?" the woman's voice continued. "Since you two fools managed to black out the entire borough of Brooklyn—"

"That was Stu's fault," the deep voice said quickly.

"It was Glen's fault," corrected the high voice.

"Quiet!" said the woman's voice. The voices were growing louder. They were coming closer and closer.

"Hurry," Lenni said as quietly but urgently as she could.

"What do you think I'm doing?" Alex whispered as he fumbled with the flashlight's switch. "Taking my time?"

Lenni grabbed the flashlight out of his hands. The little metal lever was stuck.

"Just stop worrying," the woman's voice continued, louder now. They were in the next room. "Leave all the thinking and worrying to me."

Just then, Lenni and Alex both had the same idea at the exact same moment. They both started unscrewing the small flashlight's metal base. As soon as they had the base off, the batteries came loose and the light went off at last.

That was the good news. The bad news was that one of the batteries slipped through Alex's fingers and clattered to the floor.

"We're not leaving," the woman's voice continued, "until we have every last—"

"What was that sound?" the deep voice demanded.

Now the footsteps came fast. The three thieves ran into the room. One of the three robbers, the big one, was carrying a large flashlight, which he beamed slowly around the room.

The large beam swept first one wall, then the next. Then the light moved toward the corner where Lenni and Alex were standing.

The two kids pressed back hard, as if they could move back through the wall itself.

The beam swept right past them, flashing only briefly across their faces.

"Wait," ordered the woman.

The flashlight stopped, focusing on a spot of blank wall only a few feet away.

"Back," said the woman coldly.

The flashlight came back slowly. Then it was shining right on them.

Despite the moonlight, the street outside the museum was still plenty dark. Even if it hadn't been dark, it would have been easy to miss the figure standing far back in the shadows of a doorway across the street.

Rob watched as two Con Ed workmen—one big and one little—came out the museum's metal and glass doors. The workers were carrying a huge painting.

The smaller man was in front. When he came to the step, he almost fell. Then the big man in back reached the step and almost fell as well.

"Yikes!" he yelled.

"Watch out for the step," the smaller man called.

Rob turned his back to hide the light as he clicked on the flashlight he'd bought. He shone the beam close up against his notepad, so that only a little light would spill out of the door-

83

way. The page of his notepad remained blank, as it had since he had gotten the message from Lenni about the museum.

LENNI, he wrote. ALEX, JAMAL, TINA, GABY. WHERE ARE YOU?

No answer.

We're dropping like flies, Rob thought. He shivered. He was the last fly left.

Then the letters on his notepad started to shake up and down. They sprang into a new position.

```
W  E  W  E  L  I  E  V  E

I  N  E  H  E  S  U  N  E

V  E  '  W  H  E  N  I  T

I  S  R  '  T  S  H  I  N

I  N  E  S  O  W  H  Y  I

S  I  I  S  O  H  A  R  D

T  O  N  E  L  I  E  V  E

T  H  S  T  E  V  E  R  Y

O  N  I  C  A  N  G  E  T

A  L  D  N  G  W  I  T  H

E  A  E  H  O  T  H  E  R
```

It was the same kind of crazy jumbled message as last time, Rob realized. Whichever teammate was writing to him, he or she must have been writing across another one of Q's paintings.

That meant he needed to look for the message within the message. He started moving his pen across the letters, searching for the words.

● ATTENTION, READER!
THE HIDDEN MESSAGE STARTS SOMEWHERE IN THE TOP ROW AND READS STRAIGHT DOWN. FIND IT!
—GHOSTWRITER

Rob banged his pen against the paper in frustration. Then he tried a new approach. He tried to figure out what Q's message said. He figured that the wrong letters in the message would spell out the new message.

It didn't take him long. He came up with WE WELIEVE IN EHE SUN EVE' WHEN IT ISR'T SHININE SO WHY IS II SO HARD TO NELIEVE THST EVERYONI CAN GET ALDNG WITH EAEH OTHER.

Then he circled all the wrong letters. He turned back toward the museum. WE'RE INSIDE, read the message he had circled. He started writing furiously.

WHERE INSIDE?

His letters sparkled and flew. The answer came back quickly. NO ANSWER, wrote Ghostwriter. SO WORRIED!

You're not the only one, thought Rob with a shiver. Then the letters danced on his notepad. It was another jumbled message. Why did they keep writing on Q's paintings?

This time he was able to decipher the message quickly.

THIS IS LENNI AND ALEX. WE'RE WITH GABY AND TINA.

A broad grin burst across Rob's face at the sight of the last two names. They were safe! Well, at least they were alive!

The next jumbled message wiped the smile away. WE'RE LOCKED IN BACK.

HOLD ON, Rob wrote. I'M GOING TO TRY TO CALL LIEUTENANT MCQUADE.

He watched as the two thieves carried another painting to the trucks. He waited until the men had disappeared into the museum again. Then he ran.

He found a pay phone quickly. But getting through to Lieutenant McQuade was anything but fast.

"Haven't you heard our radio bulletins?" an angry policeman asked when Rob finally got through to the station. "We're asking everyone not to use their phones until we can get power restored. We've got enough trouble with—"

"Please," Rob interrupted, "I'm begging you. Just please, please put me through to Lieutenant McQuade. If I can just talk to him for one second, I could—"

"Son, Lieutenant McQuade has about sixteen emergencies he's personally taking care of at this very moment, so—"

The policeman stopped himself mid-sentence. Rob heard the officer talking to someone else in the room. "It's some kids, Lieutenant. I don't know, I think he said something about Alex, Jamal, Lenni—oh, I'm sorry. I didn't know you would want—" The officer came back on the line. "You still there?"

"Yes!"

"Hold on."

And then Lieutenant McQuade's deep voice—wonderfully familiar—came over the wire. "Okay," the lieutenant said, after Rob blurted out the situation. "Just hold on. And don't go in the museum, understand? Do you understand?"

"Yes."

"Okay. We'll be there as fast as we can."

The line went dead.

Rob felt a moment of relief and hope. But just then a new jumbled message spun across his notepad. When he unscrambled it, his blood went cold.

ROBBERS RIGHT OUTSIDE THIS ROOM. SAY THEY DON'T WANT TO LEAVE ANY WITNESSES!

That settled it. Lieutenant McQuade had told him to stay outside, but Lieutenant McQuade didn't have the information Rob was holding in his hand right now.

The message on his notepad was jumping like crazy. The new message was from a frantic Ghostwriter. Ghostwriter agreed with Rob. His flashing message read, HURRY, ROB! NOW!

He ran back around the corner, darting in and out of doorways. Once again, he waited until the two Con Ed workers had disappeared inside the museum. He counted to ten.

And then he started across the wide street, heading toward the museum's front doors.

CHAPTER 10

BREAKOUT

Locked up in the underground transmission center, Jamal was thinking, Okay, can things get any worse than this?

He shook his head. He didn't want to know the answer to that. For the past ten minutes, he'd been reading the team's messages by flashlight. But with his pen out of ink, he couldn't answer.

He started prowling around the room, shining his flashlight into every nook and cranny. Maybe there was a pen or pencil lying around.

He didn't find a pen. Instead, he saw two beady eyes, looking bright red and shiny in the glare of his flashlight. Great, he thought, a pen with eyes.

Then he yelled and stumbled backward.

"Okay, okay, it's just a rat," he said aloud. He found it comforting to hear his own voice. "It's probably as scared of me as I am of it."

But he moved as far away from the corner where he had seen the rat as he possibly could.

As he hurried across the room, something crumpled under his feet. He was standing on a large sheet of paper.

"No," he said aloud, "I'm not looking for something to write *on*. I'm looking for something to write with."

But he picked up the paper anyway and peered at it. It was a chart. An electrical chart.

As he came into the museum lobby, Rob moved to his left, sliding along the wall. He had his flashlight off. But there was enough moonlight coming through the windows for him to see where he was going. A room in back, they had said. That didn't help much. Should he go right or left? He chose left.

He headed through the first archway into the next dark room. He was expecting the robbers to jump him any second. But room after room was empty. When he reached the last room, he figured he was in the back. And in back of this back room was another set of wooden double doors. He turned the lock, opened the doors, and moved inside.

Suddenly there were figures moving. He was surrounded.

It was dark, but he didn't need more light to recognize the

four faces that smiled back at him. Lenni, Alex, Tina, and Gaby.

"Nice going!" cried Gaby. Tina and Lenni both clapped him on the back.

Rob clicked on his flashlight. The walls of this room were covered, top to bottom, with spray-painted murals.

"That's why we wrote on the murals," Gaby explained, looking around. "There was no place else to write. I hope our messages will come off!"

"Never mind that now. Let's go," said Alex. "Let's get out of here."

"Yes, c'mon," said Lenni, leading the way.

"Wait," said Tina quietly. "The guards."

"We tried waking them up and we couldn't," Alex answered. "We can't carry them."

"The robbers could come back any second," Lenni added.

"What about Q?" asked Gaby.

"He's locked up somewhere in the museum," explained Tina.

"We can't leave him here," Gaby insisted.

The five teammates all stared at one another in the darkness. Then Rob said, "Okay. Which way?"

Jamal held his flashlight in his mouth as he studied the electrical chart. He was concentrating so hard he even stopped worrying about the rat. If only he could figure out where to plug in that blue wire. With the blackout on, he wasn't afraid of getting a shock. But first he had to figure out where the blue wire went.

"This is hopeless," whispered Lenni as the group wandered through the dark museum. "We'll never find Q. Our best bet is to get outside and wait for the cops."

"Lenni is right, I think," Rob said softly.

"Gaby," Alex called back to his sister. "Stop knocking. What's the matter with you?"

"I'm not knocking," Gaby whispered back.

"Me neither," added Tina.

"It's coming from that closet!" Lenni cried.

When they unlocked the closet door, they found Q standing inside, in the dark.

"Are you okay?" Gaby gasped.

"My whole body is asleep," he said, "but yes, I'm okay."

"We've got to be very quiet," Tina told him.

"And we've got to move fast," said Lenni.

Q was already starting toward them. "Good work, *amigos*. *Vamanos*. Let's go," he said softly.

There were six of them now, all retracing their steps through the dark rooms. Some of the rooms—the rooms without windows—were *pitch*-dark. They linked hands, forming a human chain.

"This is just like in your mural, Q," Tina whispered. "Where they put out the fire."

Q squeezed her hand more tightly.

"I don't know," Alex whispered from the front of the line. "I'm getting really nervous."

"You're *getting* nervous?" Gaby joked.

"No, I mean, we've been all through this place," Alex went on. "And no sign of them. It's too good to be true."

"Why?" Lenni said. "Maybe they left."

"And just left you guys behind?" Rob said. "I doubt it."

They were in the lobby now, where there were windows and they could see. The sight of those front doors was too much. They started running toward the doors—toward freedom.

They made it out the front door.

But then two things happened at once.

1. All over the street and in the distant skyline—everywhere but in the museum—the lights magically winked back on.

2. Three truck doors slammed. And the three thieves appeared, heading back toward the museum.

"Oh no!" cried Stu, stopping dead in his tracks. He pointed. Then he and Glen and Violet all started racing forward.

The group turned around. The only way out was to go back inside—back into the museum.

CHAPTER 11

WIRED!

"Back! Back!" shouted Alex. They were all stumbling backward.

The three thieves were halfway across the wide sidewalk.

"Lock the door!" yelled Gaby after they had all piled back into the museum. "Lock the door!"

Lenni, Q, and Tina were the last ones back inside. They fumbled with the door, looking for some kind of lock. It was hard to see in the darkness. While the street was now brightly lit, the museum was still dark.

"Lock it! Lock it!" Rob found himself shouting.

Through the lobby windows, he could see the robbers bounding up the steps, coming closer and closer. The big man, Glen, was leading the way. He reached the landing.

"The lock is electronic," Gaby said suddenly.

They all knew what that meant. With the museum power off—there was no way to keep the robbers out.

"Run!" Alex shouted.

But just then, Glen reached the door. He charged straight at it, shoulder first.

"Aha!" Jamal cried. He was in the underground power center, and he had finally found the blue wire.

He dropped it. Then he picked it up and plugged it back in. "There!" he yelled.

Throughout the museum, sirens burst into high-pitched wailing. More importantly, the lock in the front door clicked. And when Glen smashed into the metal, it didn't budge. He remained leaning against the door for a long moment. Then he said, "Ow!" as he slid slowly to the ground.

The Ghostwriter team moved to the museum windows to watch, jumping up and down, cheering wildly. Violet shook her fist at them. Then she barked an order to her men. She turned and started trotting across the street. Stu ran behind her. Glen, holding his shoulder, came last.

"They're going to get away!" yelled Tina as they watched the robbers get into their three Con Ed trucks.

"Good. Let them go," Q said.

"But your paintings!" cried Gaby.

"I can paint more paintings, *amiga,*" Q said. "This is a job for the police, not us."

He and Alex both held Gaby back as she started toward the front door. "No way, Gaby," Alex said.

The three trucks peeled out fast, with a squeal of rubber.

Tina and Gaby both groaned. But now there were more sirens adding their cries to the rest. Three police cars skidded to a halt at the end of the street, blocking the trucks. The three trucks braked with a screech, trying to make desperate U-turns.

"All right!" whooped Gaby.

Now the trucks raced back along the street the other way. But there were police cars pulling up at the other end of the block as well.

From inside the museum, they could see the furious faces of the robbers in their trucks. Violet braked and spun halfway around. Glen and Stu did not. As the Ghostwriter team cheered and laughed inside the museum lobby, Glen and Stu drove their trucks right into the truck of their boss. Glen hit the front, Stu hit the back, leaving Violet stuck in the middle.

"Sandwich!" yelled Alex.

The police got out of their cars and started toward the trucks.

EPILOGUE

"Freeze! Don't move an inch!"

Alex did as he was told.

It was two weeks later. And it was Alex's turn to pose for Q's new mural. The thieves had been caught and the paintings saved. Now the grateful artist was doing a mural portrait of the entire team on an alley wall outside the community center. His spray cans hissed as he moved his hands fast over the wall. Magically Alex's face started to appear.

The rest of the team stood watching. "Make sure you show in your painting that I am fearless," Alex told Q.

"Stop talking so much," Q answered with a chuckle. "You're moving your head."

"Remember, Q. Fearless," Alex said again.

"Don't listen to him," called Jamal with a happy laugh.

Just then Gaby came around the corner. "Alex," she called, "Mom asked me to remind you that she made your new dentist appointment for four o'clock this afternoon."

Alex made a horrible face as everyone laughed. Q laughed as well. "She's got you, Alex."

Alex shook his head, then remembered he was supposed to keep his head still. "I'm not scared of the dentist," he called to his friends.

Lenni snorted.

"I'm not," Alex insisted. "And you want to know why? Because I have a plan. Jamal," he said, "do you still have that electrical chart?"

"Yeah."

"And the rest of you still have your flashlights? Okay, good," Alex said, lowering his voice. "Here's what we do. At exactly four o'clock . . . "

From the Hit TV Show

Ghost writer

Created by CTW

BECOME AN OFFICIAL
GHOSTWRITER READERS CLUB MEMBER!

You'll receive the following GHOSTWRITER Readers Club Materials:
Official Membership Card • The Scoop on GHOSTWRITER •
GHOSTWRITER Magazine
All members registered by December 31st will have a chance to win
a FREE COMPUTER and other exciting prizes!

OFFICIAL ENTRY FORM
Mail your completed entry to: Bantam Doubleday Dell BFYR, GW Club, 1540 Broadway, New York, NY 10036

Name

Address

City   **State**   **Zip**

Age   **Phone**

---

ghost writer

MORE FUN-FILLED GHOSTWRITER BOOKS

☐ **A MATCH OF WILLS**   29934-4
by Eric Weiner $2.99/$3.50 in Canada

☐ **THE GHOSTWRITER DETECTIVE GUIDE:**   48069-3
Tools and Tricks of the Trade
by Susan Lurie $2.99/$3.50 in Canada

☐ **COURTING DANGER AND OTHER STORIES**   48070-7
by Dina Anastasio $2.99/$3.50 in Canada

☐ **DRESS CODE MESS**   48071-5
by Sara St. Antoine $2.99/$3.50 in Canada

☐ **THE BIG BOOK OF KIDS' PUZZLES**   37074-X
by P.C. Russell Ginns $1.25/$1.50 in Canada

☐ **THE MINI BOOK OF KIDS' PUZZLES**   37073-1
by Denise Lewis Patrick $.99/$1.25 in Canada

**Bantam Books, Dept DA56, 2451 South Wolf Road, Des Plaines
IL 60018**
Please send me the items I have checked above. I am enclos-
ing $ _____ (please add $2.50 to cover postage and handling)
Send check or money order, no cash or C.O.D's please.

Mr/Mrs_____

Address_____

City/State_____ Zip_____

Please allow four to six weeks for delivery.
Prices and availability subject to change without notice.   DA56 11/92